HORSE

EMILY ARNOLD McCULLY

HENRY HOLT AND COMPANY
NEW YORK

BILL KEY was born a slave on a plantation in 1833. Even as a little boy, he had a special way with animals. He could soothe and he could cure just about any creature.

After Bill grew up and slaves were freed, he became a veterinarian. He was called Doc Key. Most of his patients were horses. In those days, horses did the hauling, pulling, and carrying, and they were often abused. Few people realized that animals had feelings. Bill believed in treating every animal with kindness.

"Put down your whip!" he would say to a farmer trying to get his tired horse to move. Bill stroked the spot on the animal's neck where its mother had once nuzzled.

"All creatures like kindness," Bill advised.

His methods worked. His reputation spread.

Doc created a medicine called Keystone Liniment.
It worked on colic, lameness, cramps, and headache—in
both humans and animals. His liniment made him rich!
Doc bought a hotel and a restaurant. After he bought a
racetrack, he wanted to own the fastest horse in the country.

One day he heard that a circus was selling its animals.
Doc went to see if a racer was among them. He noticed a
beautiful mare with a distinctive profile. *An Arabian!* Doc
thought. Arabians were known for speed and intelligence.
But she looked frightened. There were marks on her flanks
where she'd been whipped.

Doc bought her for forty dollars.

Doc loved his new horse, Lauretta. She was the smartest horse he'd ever known. He found a champion stallion to father her foal. Then he waited for his future champion to be born.

But the new foal had twisted legs and a mottled, homely coat. Doc thought the foal was too weak to survive, so he called him plain old "Jim Key."

Worse, the birth used up Lauretta's strength. Doc tried desperately to save her, but Lauretta died. Doc's heart closed shut with grief.

No one could console him, not even his dogs, who waited for Doc to throw a stick for them to fetch.

Meanwhile, little Jim Key tried desperately to stand on his crooked legs. His bright black eyes begged Doc not to lose hope in him.

One day Doc felt a nudge on his shoulder. It was Jim Key, with a stick in his mouth!

"You want to play fetch?" Doc smiled for the first time in weeks. He threw the stick and Jim stumbled after it. The foal had never taken more than two steps!

Jim picked up the stick and tottered back. He trotted a
few feet! Offering the stick, he spread his lips in a grin.
"You're trying to cheer me up, aren't you?" Doc asked.

After Doc and the dogs went inside his house, he heard
loud knocking on the front door. It was Jim.

"Okay, Jim, you win," Doc said. He made Jim a bed on
the floor of the spare room. The colt slept there every night
until he was too big for the doorways and too heavy for the
floorboards. Then Doc took his own bed out to the barn.

Almost everything Doc did, Jim tried to do too. Jim figured out how to unlock the paddock gate. He opened the drawer where Doc kept apples, ate them all, and then shut the drawer. When Doc laughed at his antics, Jim seemed to laugh too.

"I wonder what else you could learn," Doc said. Jim lifted his chin as if to say "Try me!" Doc decided to take time off from selling liniment.

Doc taught Jim one lesson at a time, repeating it and rewarding Jim with apples or sugar. First, Doc wrote the letter A on a card. He said "A" aloud, then put the card in Jim's lips, held them shut, and patted his neck.

It took many months, but Doc never lost patience. Finally, when Doc asked Jim to fetch the "A," Jim did it.

They proceeded to B, then to C, until
Jim knew the whole alphabet.

In the following years, Jim learned to
count and to pick out the primary colors.

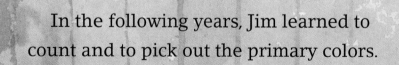

One day, watching Jim add and subtract, Doc cried, "Jim, we should go on the road! People will be amazed by how much you know. They will see that animals have feelings, and it's wrong to make them suffer."

"Wonder if Jim can do that in front of strangers," one of Doc's farmhands said. "Might just be sensing what you want him to do, not learning at all."

Doc knew that Jim had truly been educated. He arranged for a show to prove it.

At first, audiences couldn't believe their eyes. But soon they were gasping and cheering. Jim Key loved being the star of the show. The bigger the audience, the more he hammed it up.

Jim spelled, made change from a cash register, danced
to music, and bowed to ladies in the audience, flicking his
tail and grinning.

Jim and Doc traveled to fairs, small town theaters, and big city arenas.

But one day, Doc saw a newspaper headline: "Is Horse's Intelligence a Fraud?" The story asked, "How could a little old black man with no education teach a dumb animal to do those things?"

The next day, there were hecklers in the audience. "This is all a trick!" one shouted.

"Some people are offended by your brainpower," Doc said to Jim. "But children believe in you."

Doc asked the local board of education to close the schools for a day so that every child in town could come to the show.

The board replied, "We can't close our schools for horse shows or monkey shows."

The insult made Doc more determined. "Jim, we have to find a sponsor. We can't fight prejudice all by ourselves."

Doc wrote to the Society for the Prevention of Cruelty to Animals. "Let us team up. Jim can help spread your message."

"What if your act is a hoax?" they wrote back. "People already call us foolish for teaching kindness to animals."

Doc invited them to come see for themselves, and they agreed, as long as the demonstration was secret.

The big day arrived. Doc and Jim waited and waited but no one showed up.

Doc said, "I have another idea."

Doc invited a team of professors from Harvard University to examine Jim Key and decide if he was really educated. The professors agreed.

"You must wait outside while we examine Jim," they told Doc.

They led Jim inside and shut the door. Doc waited patiently. A crowd gathered.

Hours later, the door opened. The professors announced their findings:

"It is not a hoax. Jim answered all of our questions. He can read, spell, do arithmetic, and identify colors entirely as a result of his education."

Every newspaper carried the story:

JIM KEY EDUCATED BY KINDNESS.

The Society for the Prevention of
Cruelty to Animals agreed to sponsor
Jim Key's performances. After the shows,
thousands of schoolchildren signed
a pledge that said "I promise to treat
animals with kindness."

For nine years, Doc and Jim Key traveled the country in a custom railroad car, delighting audiences of all kinds. Then they retired to a peaceful life on Jim Key Farm, where enthusiastic fans visited, and Jim was always happy to amaze them with what he knew.

AUTHOR'S NOTE

Courtesy of the Tennessee State Library and Archives

This story is based upon the real lives of Bill Key and Jim Key.

Born in slavery in 1833, Bill "Doc" Key became a doctor to humans and animals even before the Civil War. During the war he saved the lives of his master's two sons, following them into battle with Confederate troops. Accused of being a spy, he escaped hanging by using his wits, his skill as a chef, and his unsurpassed poker playing.

After he was freed by the Emancipation Proclamation, Doc Key used his own money to pay off his master's mortgage. His success as a vet with a medicine show is all the more remarkable for the dangers he faced in the Jim Crow South. By calling attention to himself, traveling, speaking to crowds, and amassing a fortune, he risked harm or even death at the hands of the Ku Klux Klan, which was founded in Doc's home state of Tennessee. Doc Key did suffer the racist humiliation and ridicule widely tolerated throughout the United States during Reconstruction and for long afterward. He died in 1909.

Jim Key was born in 1889. He performed in Doc's medicine show—feigning illness, then recovering after a dose of Keystone Liniment—until he debuted with a higher education at the Tennessee Centennial Exhibition in 1897. Jim's extraordinary climb to superstardom reached its apex at the 1904 St. Louis World's Fair. He died in 1912 and is buried near Shelbyville, Tennessee, where a memorial to Jim and Doc Key stands today.

While Jim's performances were amazing, Doc Key's skill as a trainer was even more so. Over seven years of tireless repetition, he taught Jim to recognize letters and numbers and to combine them in response to questions. Jim also performed in skits.

Some in the humane movement were afraid to associate themselves with Jim Key. But George Angell, founder of the Massachusetts Society for the Prevention of Cruelty to Animals, was a supporter. He may have asked the Harvard professors to examine the educated horse. They probably watched Jim perform and interviewed Doc but didn't do controlled experiments. A horse named Clever Hans, who lived in Germany at about the same time, was found to respond to his trainer's unconscious cues when performing "mental" feats. Apparently this hypothesis wasn't tested in Jim's case.

Scientists are still trying to define "animal intelligence." The story of Jim Key proves that human patience and kindness can dramatically stimulate it.

BIBLIOGRAPHY

"Could Your Horse Pass the Mensa Test? Psychology Researcher Proves That Horses Can Count!" *The Jurga Report: Horse Health Headlines*. Available from special.equisearch.com/blog/horsehealth/labels/Beautiful%20Jim%20Key.html.

"Equine prodigies: Clever Hans; Lady Wonder; and Beautiful Jim Key." Available from bridlepath.wordpress.com/?s=jim+key.

Key, John F. "A Master's Tribute to a Slave of Ante-Bellum Days." *Washington Times*, July 13, 1903, national edition. Available from www.loc.gov/chroniclingamerica/lccn/sn84026749/1903-07-13/ed-1/seq-7.

Lee, Essie Mott. *The Man Who Educated a Horse (A Pioneer in Humane Education)*. Bloomington, IN: 1st Books Library, 1998.

Rivas, Mim Eichler. *Beautiful Jim Key: The Lost History of a Horse and a Man Who Changed the World*. New York: William Morrow, 2005.

———. *Beautiful Jim Key*. Available from www.beautifuljimkey.com.

St. Louis Public Library. "Celebrating the Louisiana Purchase (1904 World's Fair)—The Horse That Counted." Available from exhibits.slpl.org/lpe/data/lpe240023588.asp?Image=43996475.

Henry Holt and Company, LLC, *Publishers since 1866*
175 Fifth Avenue, New York, New York 10010
www.HenryHoltKids.com

Henry Holt® is a registered trademark of Henry Holt and Company, LLC.
Copyright © 2010 by Emily Arnold McCully
All rights reserved.
Distributed in Canada by H. B. Fenn and Company Ltd.

Library of Congress Cataloging-in-Publication Data
McCully, Emily Arnold.
Wonder horse : the true story of the world's smartest horse / Emily Arnold McCully. — 1st ed.
p. cm.
Summary: A fictionalized account of Bill "Doc" Key, a former slave who became a veterinarian, trained his horse, Jim Key, to recognize letters and numbers and to perform in skits around the country, and moved the nation toward a belief in treating animals humanely. Includes an author's note. Includes bibliographical references.
ISBN 978-0-8050-8793-2
1. Key, Bill, 1833–1909—Juvenile fiction. [1. Key, Bill, 1833–1909—Fiction. 2. Horses—Training—Fiction. 3. African Americans—Fiction.] I. Title.
PZ7.M478415Wo 2010   [E]—dc22   2009006208

First Edition—2010 / Designed by April Ward
Printed in October 2009 in China by Imago USA Inc., Dongguan City, Guangdong Province, on acid-free paper. ∞

10 9 8 7 6 5 4 3 2 1